Behind the Back of the Mountain

Behind the Back of the Mountain

Black Folktales from Southern Africa
Retold by Verna Aardema · *Pictures by Leo and*
Diane Dillon · *The Dial Press, New York*

Library of Congress Cataloging in Publication Data
Aardema, Verna. Behind the back of the mountain.
Summary: Ten folk legends from southern Africa include
Hottentot, Zulu, and Bantu tales.
Bibliography: p.   1. Tales, African—Africa, Southern.
[1. Folklore—Africa, Southern] I. Dillon, Leo, illus. II. Dillon,
Diane, illus. III. Title. PZ8.1.A213Be   398.2'0968   72-7602

For little Kristin Aardema,
who tells stories to me

A hundred years ago the Bushman storyteller, Hiddoro Kabbo, said that when one has traveled along a road he can sit down and wait for a story to overtake him. He said a story is like the wind. It comes from a far place and it can pass behind the back of a mountain.

Here, one has only to turn the page to allow a story to overtake him.

V. A.

Contents

Behind the Back of the Mountain

A Zulu Tale

Little Hen Eagle

Beyond the mountain there once lived a chief who had three children by his Great Wife. The oldest was Bead Woman, who was the wife of a king in a distant village. Next was Usilwane, who was a young man. And last was Little Hen Eagle, who was not quite grown-up.

One day Usilwane returned from hunting with a small leopard cub which he named Long Wedding Song. He told his mother, "This will be my dog. When he grows up, I will hunt with him. Make porridge for him. But be sure it is cold before you feed him, for he will die if he eats hot food."

The people of the village were afraid of the leopard.

They said, "Why does the son of our chief tame a leopard and call him his dog?"

Little Hen Eagle was afraid of the animal too. She feared that some night he might remember that he was a leopard and attack her as she slept.

One day Usilwane and his sister were alone in the village. The rest of the people were hunting or working at their farms. The brother said, "I'm going for a walk in the forest. Feed Long Wedding Song while I'm gone. But remember to let the food cool before you give it to him."

After Usilwane had gone, Little Hen Eagle boiled ground corn and milk. And while it was still hot, she fed it to the leopard. The animal gobbled it up, then lay down and died.

When Usilwane returned at midday, he saw that his leopard was dead. He cried, "Little Hen Eagle, did you kill my dog?"

"The porridge must have been a little too hot," she said.

"You killed him on purpose!" cried Usilwane.

Little Hen Eagle ran out the door and down the path toward their father's farm. Usilwane snatched up his sword and set out after her. She outran him for a little way. But when she saw that he was catching up with her, she gasped out a little prayer: "Earth, open for me!"

At once a tunnel opened before her. She leaped into it. Then the earth closed behind her, with every blade of grass back in place.

4

When Usilwane reached the spot, he said, "Where did she go? She was here. I saw her!" But he could find no trace of her, so he went home.

The tunnel led Little Hen Eagle to the middle of the chief's farm. When she emerged, she ran to her mother and said, "Mother, Usilwane is trying to kill me!"

"He wouldn't do that," said her mother.

"But I killed his leopard," said Little Hen Eagle. "I fed him hot porridge!"

"In that case," said the mother, "you'd better go and stay with Bead Woman until his anger has cooled."

"But Bead Woman has been gone so long, I won't know her," said Little Hen Eagle. "And she won't know me."

"She will remember your name," said the mother. Then she commanded her maidservant, Dog Tail, to fetch an ox for Little Hen Eagle to ride. She told Dog Tail to lead the ox, and she taught her the roads to follow to the village of Bead Woman.

The two set out. Little Hen Eagle looked like the princess she was in her clean calfskin dress and her bracelets and bangles of brass. But Dog Tail had had no time to prepare for the journey. She had to wear the dirty, shabby garment she had worn at work on the farm.

They traveled for two days, and at length came to a river. There they took off their clothes and bathed. Dog Tail hurried and finished first. Then she put on Little Hen Eagle's

6

dress and her brass ornaments, and hastily mounted the ox.

When Little Hen Eagle came out of the water, there was nothing for her to put on but Dog Tail's shabby things. She stamped her foot and cried, "Dog Tail, give me my clothes!"

"Why should I?" said Dog Tail. "I am clean and just as pretty as you. Your sister won't know the difference. Now you are Dog Tail, and I am Little Hen Eagle." She laughed in a most annoying way. Then she continued, "But I'm too big to be called Little. I'll just be Hen Eagle. And you're too little to be called Dog Tail. You will be Puppy Tail."

There was nothing for Little Hen Eagle to do but put on the ragged garments and lead the ox.

At sundown they arrived at the village of Bead Woman. Dog Tail made Little Hen Eagle hold the ox outside the gate. Then she went to the queen and said, "I am your sister, Hen Eagle. Our mother has sent me to visit you."

Bead Woman said, "My sister was a baby when I left home. How can she have grown so big? And her name was *Little* Hen Eagle."

"I know," said the false sister, "but I'm too big to be called that now. Now people just call me Hen Eagle."

Bead Woman prepared food for her and said, "Call your servant yonder that she may eat also."

"Feed Puppy Tail outside," said Hen Eagle.

The queen called her servant, Udalana, and told her to give Puppy Tail something to eat and take her to her hut.

But Hen Eagle was given one of the houses of the royal family.

The next morning Puppy Tail went with Udalana to help drive the birds out of the queen's garden. There were two watch-houses, one on either side. One of the girls went to each.

When a flock of birds came fluttering down to the garden, Udalana threw stones at them. The birds paid little attention to the stones. Then Puppy Tail sang:

> "Tayi, tayi. Listen to me.
> Fly away birds. Tayi, tayi."

The birds flew off at once. After that Udalana didn't have to throw another stone, for Puppy Tail chased the birds away with her magic song.

At midday Puppy Tail went to the river to bathe. Udalana followed her and hid in the bushes to see what strange thing she might do next. The girl was not disappointed. For when Puppy Tail finished bathing, she came out of the water carrying a shiny brass rod. She struck the earth with it and said, "Come forth, my parents and all my things."

At once the earth opened and out came her father and mother, an ox, and fine ornaments and clothing. Puppy Tail dressed herself in the royal garments and mounted the ox. Then with her father on one side and her mother on the other, she sang:

9

> "In my father's cattlefold we sang, E-a-ye;
> To the white-tailed cattle we sang, E-a-ye;
> To the red-tailed cattle we sang, E-a-ye."

She repeated the song. And this time the parents and even the ox sang with her. Then she dismounted, took off the fine clothing, and put down the brass rod. As suddenly as they had appeared, all were swallowed up by the earth. Then Puppy Tail put on her ragged garments and returned to the garden.

That night Udalana told the king what she had seen. He told Bead Woman, and the two went to see Puppy Tail. The king said, "Udalana has told us that you have magic power. Who are you?"

"I am the real Little Hen Eagle," she said. Then she told how she had killed Usilwane's leopard, and how he had chased her with his sword. She told how Dog Tail had taken her garments and had taken her name as well.

Bead Woman embraced her and said, "My sister! That wicked one shall be punished!"

"Don't punish her," said Little Hen Eagle. "Send her back to our father's village with a dog for Usilwane. Then perhaps he will no longer hate me."

So Dog Tail took a hunting dog to Usilwane. He forgave his sister. And after a long visit with Bead Woman, Little Hen Eagle went home too.

A Bushman Tale

The Trick on the Trek

Near the southwest coast of Africa there is a shallow river that wanders slowly to the sea. One dry season the water in it became so low that the river could hardly flow.

The lungfish buried themselves in the mud to sleep until the rains returned. The otters could find no pools deep enough for diving. And the crocodiles found themselves half-way out of the water, in plain view of any elephant who might decide to flip one of them into a nearby tree. It was embarrassing and dangerous.

One morning the crocodile, who was chief of all the water animals, called the otter to her. She said, "Scout out the country to the south of us. See if you can find a deep river to which we can move."

The otter set out at once, and returned the next day. He told the crocodile, "We are in luck! There's a river out there so deep that sea cows are living in its deepest pools."

"Good!" cried the crocodile. "We will go to it."

"That will not be easy," said the otter. "Between here and there are forests and fields infested with lions and elephants. And worse than that, there is a farm with many men working in the fields, and a pen full of dogs that bark at everything that passes."

"Where there are men, there are spears," said the crocodile. "But we must go. Lion should know how to get past the farm. We will make peace with him and ask him to help us."

"How can we make peace with Lion?" asked the otter.

"Take a message to him," said the crocodile.

The otter said, "But to Lion everything that runs is food. He would have my head off before I finished speaking."

A turtle had been sunning himself on a nearby sandbar. He lumbered over and said, "Lion won't eat me. I'll take the message."

"Well spoken!" cried the crocodile. "Tell Lion to meet me at dusk under the giant willow yonder. Tell him I want to talk about a matter of life and death for both the land and water animals."

12

The turtle delivered the message to the lion. The lion said, "M-m-m, I must consult with Jackal. But in any case, tell your chief that we will meet her under the big willow at sundown."

The crocodile was pleased when she heard that the lion had agreed to come. She ordered the otter to have plenty of fish and crabs prepared for the guests to eat.

When the lion and the jackal arrived, they were treated in a most friendly manner. After they had eaten, the crocodile told them about the sad plight of the water creatures. She asked the lion to provide protection for them as they trekked to the river of the sea cow pools.

After such a good meal, the lion would have agreed to anything. But the jackal asked, "What benefit shall we land animals receive if we help you?"

"Peace would benefit both sides," said the crocodile. "We will no longer try to kill each other. When you land animals come to drink, we will no longer try to seize you by the nose. You will be able to drink without fear."

"Good!" said the lion. "It's dreadful to feel that one's life is in danger every time he puts his mouth into the water to drink."

"From your side," continued the crocodile, "you must free us from the fear of elephants. They have the habit of tossing us up into the treetops and leaving us to hang till we become *biltong*."

13

Then the lion wanted to know what security the crocodile would give that the agreement would be kept. She said, "I give you my word," and she let fall a few tears of honesty.

The lion and the jackal stepped aside to consult with one another. They agreed that this would never have come about if the crocodiles were not in a tight spot, and that the chance for peace might never come again.

The lion said, "We agree. I will gather an escort for you. We shall meet you here at moonrise."

"Thank you, thank you," said the crocodile. "We shall be ready. Arrange your guards any way you like, but I would appreciate having elephants protect the rear."

The lion saw no reason to argue about that. He agreed readily, and set off with the jackal to gather the land animals.

Meanwhile the crocodile's messengers went up and down the river assembling the water animals who wanted to make the journey. Soon hundreds of crocodiles, otters, turtles, frogs, and crabs were gathered near the huge willow.

As the moon came up over the trees, the lion arrived with his subjects. He looked out over the mass of water animals waiting shoulder to shoulder to begin the march. He placed a row of jackals as the advance guard.

The chief of the jackals said, "I don't trust crocodiles! I'll lead the way past the farm. But then we jackals will leave."

The lion laughed. He didn't blame the jackal for being jumpy with an army of crocodiles behind him. The lion placed a troop of baboons on the left flank, and a dozen lions on the right. Then as the crocodile had suggested, he ordered the elephants to guard the rear.

While all this was going on, the crocodile chief was quietly preparing a trick. She didn't believe that the lion could make the elephants let the crocodiles alone. And she wanted to get even with them for past crimes.

The crocodile hunted up a yellow snake and said to him, "It is to our advantage to have these elephants fall into the hands of the farmer and his men. You follow along behind the trek and linger near the farm. When you hear me shout, you will know that we water animals have safely reached the big river. Then you must wake the dogs. The rest will happen by itself."

The crocodile took her place behind the jackals, and the company began to move. It was necessary to go slowly, as many of the water animals had difficulty traveling on land. The noise of their moving was like a steady wind in a mealie patch.

The animals were downwind from the farm, and they managed to pass it without wakening the dogs. At dawn they reached the deep river. The water creatures all tumbled into it.

The crocodile turned to the lion and the other land animals and said, "Thank you for your help. I am so happy, I could shout!" She opened her huge mouth and bellowed so

that the sound echoed. Then she thanked them again, making a long speech of it.

The lion had just begun to make a speech in reply when an elephant trumpeted a cry of alarm.

Suddenly the air was filled with flying spears and poison arrows as the farmer and his men attacked. The crocodile slipped into the water, leaving the battle behind her. Only elephants were killed, since the jackals had already left, and the baboons and lions escaped into the bush on either side.

And that was the end of the peace treaty.

For even to this day, when an elephant gets the chance, he pitches a crocodile up into the fork of a tree. And crocodiles still sneak up and seize drinking animals by the nose, drag them into the deep water, and drown them.

A Tshindao Tale

Tshinyama's Heavenly Maidens

Near the Enyati Mountains there once lived a young man named Tshinyama, which means skin sore. He was called that because his skin was spotted with sores.

One day Tshinyama set out to find a wife. His brother said, "How can *you* get a wife? Girls run from you. And who would give his daughter to a man with skin sores?"

Nevertheless, Tshinyama set out on his quest. Before long he came to a beautiful pool. It was fed by a bubbling spring and ringed about with reeds and blossoming mimosa trees.

Tshinyama sat down under a tree to rest. Soon he was startled by the sound of flapping wings. He looked up and saw two heavenly maidens descending from the sky. He crept away and hid himself in a thicket. From his hiding place, he saw the strange creatures alight at the water's edge. They were lovely beyond belief. Their bodies were the color of bronze, and their white wings were edged with gold.

Tshinyama watched as they took off the wings and spread them on a nearby rock. Then, with squeals of delight, they plunged into the cool water. While they played in the pool, the young man stole their wings.

When the maidens finished bathing and found their wings were gone, they began to weep. Tshinyama stepped out of the reeds and said, "Do not cry, pretty maidens. I have your wings. What will you do for me if I give them back to you?"

The taller of the two said, "Give us our wings and my sister and I will marry you."

"Come to my father's *kraal* and marry me first," said the youth.

The smaller sister demanded, "How could we appear before your parents without our wings?"

Both of them insisted upon getting their wings first. Tshinyama thought that creatures who looked so beautiful could not break a promise. So he gave them their wings. He even helped to fasten them onto their shoulders. No sooner was this done than the taller one said, "Come, Sister!" And the two spread their wings and flew away up into the sky.

The next day Tshinyama hid near the pool to see if the

sisters would return. They did. Again he stole their wings while they bathed. This time he carried them back to his village and hid them there. When he returned to the pool, he found the maidens weeping.

Tshinyama said, "It is I who have taken your wings. This time I won't give them back to you until after you marry me."

There was nothing for the sisters to do but go back with Tshinyama to his *kraal*. On the way he named the tall one Tiye, which means hatred. The small one he called Imfi, which means sugar cane.

When the people of the village saw Tshinyama with the two lovely young women, they gathered around and said, "Tshinyama, where did you get those wives?"

"I found them," is all he would answer.

Two behive-shaped houses were built for Tiye and Imfi. They learned to cook and to work in the gardens. But they were not happy, for their husband refused to give them their wings. He would say, "When I gave them to you before, you flew away. Some day you shall have them, but not today."

One day Imfi said to him, "Please, Husband, give us our wings so we can visit our parents in their *kraal* in the sky. You can come with us. We will carry you."

"Very well," said Tshinyama. He fetched the wings and helped fasten them on. Then Tiye clasped his right hand

and Imfi his left, and they flew with him up into the sky.

When they reached their home in the heavens, the young wives flew into the arms of their parents. The mother and father were delighted to see them. But when the father's eyes fell on Tshinyama, he cried, "What kind of man is this? He has no wings, and his skin is covered with sores. Fetch the cooking pot! We shall cut him up and make medicine of him!"

"No, no," cried Imfi. "He is our husband!"

"That's right," said Tiye. "He is our husband and he loves us. Tomorrow we shall carry him back to our village on the earth."

That night as Tshinyama lay on a mat in the guest hut, a rat came to him and said, "When your father-in-law calls you in the morning, do not go to him. He plans to kill you and make you into medicine."

"Tiye and Imfe won't let him do that," said Tshinyama.

But the rat said, "I heard them talking. Your wives have already given their consent."

Tshinyama did not sleep all night. At the very first streak of dawn, he slipped out of the hut and ran along a path which led away from the village.

Soon he met the rat who had warned him. It ran along beside him. Farther on the two came upon an aardvark and a spider. Tshinyama said, "Friends, I wish to return to my *kraal* on the earth. Can you help me?"

"If we should," said the rat, "what would you give us as a reward?"

"Whatever you wish," said the young man.

The rat said he wanted porridge scrapings; the spider wanted flies; and the aardvark, an ant hill. Tshinyama promised to give them those things.

So the aardvark bored a hole through the floor of the sky with his snout. Then the spider spun a silken cord, on which they all climbed down. When they reached the earth, Tshinyama gave the animals the things they had asked for, and they went away.

The next morning Tshinyama hid in the reeds by the pool, hoping the heavenly maidens would return. They did not come.

Every day thereafter, Tshinyama waited near that pool. And one morning Tiye and Imfi did return. While they bathed, Tshinyama took their wings. When they looked for them, he stepped out and said, "I have your wings and I'll never give them back to you. You belong to me, and you shall not fly away again." Then he built a fire and burned the wings.

In time Tiye and Imfi became accustomed to the earth, and were satisfied to live as earthlings. One day as they were returning from their garden, they found a rare medicinal plant. They gathered some of its leaves. When they reached the village, they filled a huge pot with water and built a fire around it. Then they threw in the leaves.

When Tshinyama came home, Tiye said, "Husband, climb into the pot."

Tshinyama backed away, crying, "What have I done that you should make medicine of me?"

Imfi doubled over with laughter. "We aren't going to make medicine of you!" she cried. "There is medicine in the pot. Get in. It will heal you."

Tshinyama felt the water. It was not too hot. So he climbed into the pot and splashed the yellow water all over himself. Then a wonderful thing happened. The sores were drawn out of his skin. When his wives helped him out, his skin was smooth and beautiful.

Tshinyama was so happy that he laughed a big booming laugh. Because of that, he was no longer called Tshinyama. He was called Mahleka, which means laughter.

A Hottentot Tale

How Blue Crane Taught Jackal To Fly

High in a gwenye tree near the edge of the Kalahari Desert there once lived a dove and her two fat babies.

One day when the sun was at its peak, the dove sat on the rim of her nest of sticks with her wings spread out to shade her children. She was singing in a sleepy voice:

> "Coo-wee-ooo,
> Coo-wee-ooo.
> Mother is making
> A shadow for you.
> Aardwolf and lizard

26

Are resting too.
Coo-wee-ooo,
Coo-wee-ooo."

A jackal passing under the tree heard the dove singing and called, "*Heyi!* Daughter of my sister, what is the meaning of your song?"

"Uncle," replied the dove, "I am singing to my children so they will not beg for food during the heat of the day."

"Your song is sweet," said the jackal. "How many children have you?"

"Two, two, two," cooed the dove.

The jackal ran around the tree to see if anyone was looking, and came back to his place under the nest. Then he said, "Dove, I'm very hungry! Throw down one of your children for me to eat. Then you'll only have one to feed."

"No!" cried the dove. "Both of my children are dear to me. Get your food where you are in the habit of finding it."

The jackal drew in his breath to make his ribs stand out. "Can you who are so gentle sit there and see a person starve?" he demanded.

"I'm sorry for you, Jackal," said the dove. "But go away. You're disturbing my children with your talk."

Then the jackal sprang up in a rage and cried, "Throw down one of your children or I'll come up there and eat both of them!"

27

The dove was so frightened that she forgot that a jackal cannot climb a tree. To save one of the babies she threw the other one down.

The jackal ate it in one bite. Then he ran around the tree to see if anyone was looking. "Dove," he called again, "how many babies have you?"

"Only one, one, one," mourned the dove.

"Throw it down to me," cried the jackal, "or I'll climb up and get it. And I'll eat you and the nest of sticks too!" Then the jackal scrabbled a little way up the rough trunk of the tree as if he were beginning to climb it.

The dove was so frightened that she threw down the other baby. The jackal ate it and went on his way.

The mother dove looked into her empty nest and moaned, "Woo, woo, woo! What have I done?"

A blue crane happened along. He listened to the crying of the dove. Then he asked, "Little Sister, why are you so sad?"

The dove told him all about it. The crane tipped his head sideways so that one eye was looking up at the dove. He said, "You were safe in your nest. Who told you a jackal can climb a tree?"

"He did," said the dove. "I believed him, and now my babies are gone."

The blue crane lifted his wings a little and put them down, as is the manner of cranes when they are thinking. Then he said, "Jackal made you believe he could climb a tree. I'll make *him* believe he can learn to fly!" With that, he strode off chuckling softly to himself.

The big bird did not find the jackal that day. But a few days later he happened to meet him. The jackal's tongue was lolling out of his mouth, and he looked as though he had been running fast and far.

The blue crane said, "Jackal, rest a bit! You'll run yourself to death one of these days!"

The jackal stopped and said, "Grandfather, haven't you noticed? A big storm is coming. I want to get back to my den before it breaks."

"Hurry on, then," said the blue crane, spreading his wings as though he were about to fly away. "You animals who have to run along on the ground are to be pitied. To us who fly, long distances are nothing."

"You're right!" said the jackal. "I have always envied you creatures of the wide wings."

"Meet me here when the storm is over," said the bird. "I'll teach you to fly."

The jackal promised to return, then scurried off through the thornbushes.

When the storm was over the jackal met the blue crane at the appointed place. He sat at the edge of a thicket while the crane strode back and forth before him. "If you really want to learn to fly," said the bird, "you must do everything I tell you to do."

"Of course," said the jackal. "Get on with it."

"See that mimosa tree with the gum dripping from it?" said the blue crane. "Go to that tree and rub the gum all over yourself."

The jackal did that, and came back saying, "This learning to fly is not pleasant. All my hair sticks together in a most uncomfortable way!"

The blue crane said nothing, but began to pluck feathers from himself and stick them into the gum with which the jackal was covered. He worked until the animal's body was clothed with feathers. Then he plucked a long feather from his tail and stuck that on the jackal's tail.

The jackal was delighted. He stood up on his hind legs and flapped his front paws. "*Kwowu!*" he cried. "I *am* a bird!" Then he ran on two legs, flapping his front paws as hard as he could. But he was not able to get off the ground.

"What trick is this?" he demanded. "You made me into a bird that can't fly."

The blue crane laughed. "You're in too much of a hurry," he said. "I'll teach you to fly the way I teach my children. Get on my back. I'll take you high into the air. When I give the word, you must jump off and fly. That is how my children learn."

The jackal looked up at the sky and down to the ground.

"You aren't afraid, are you?" asked the crane.

"No, no," said the jackal. "I was just measuring the height of the sky." Then he climbed upon the crane's back. When he was firmly settled the big bird ran a little way, then spread his wings and rose up, up high into the air. He flew so high that the houses looked like fat brown beetles, and the women at work in the fields looked like ants.

They were above a farm when the blue crane said, "Get ready! Jump!" At the same moment, he withdrew himself from under the jackal.

The jackal tried to fly with all four feet. But he plummeted toward the earth with the feathers trailing behind him. He soon forgot to kick, and put all his energy into one long howl.

When the women in the field heard the voice from the sky and saw the strange thing falling toward them, they dropped their hoes and ran. Jackal fell upon a hoe. And there he died.

Then the blue crane went back to the dove and told her the story of how the jackal learned to fly.

A Zulu Tale

The Winning of Kwelanga

Near the Mountains of the Dragon, there once lived a great chief named Ngazulu. He had a daughter who was so beautiful and gentle that she was called Kwelanga, which means sunrise.

It was the chief's desire that Kwelanga be married to a man worthy of her. So all suitors were put to impossible tests. Naturally all failed to win her.

One day a young man named Zamo heard about this. At once he decided to try his luck. His father tried to dissuade him. He said, "We are poor people. How dare you think of marrying the daughter of the chief?"

34

His mother said, "Oh, Zamo! Every man who has tried has lost his life. Do you think you would fare any better?"

But Zamo said, "I can't whistle with another man's mouth. I must try it myself."

So one day Zamo went to Chief Ngazulu and said, "Greetings, *Nkosi*." Then he waited for the chief to speak.

The chief said, "Young man, what are you doing here? Have you lost your way?"

"No, *Nkosi*," said Zamo. "This is the end of my journey. I have come to propose marriage with your daughter."

"*You* come, with no attendants, to propose marriage?" cried the chief.

"*Nkosi*," said Zamo humbly, "it is the custom of my people to act alone."

"Proposer-of-marriage," said the chief, "are you prepared to do the tasks we will set for you?"

"I am here to try," said Zamo.

Ngazulu said, "Well then, look yonder. Do you see that cultivated field? Kaffir corn has been sown there. Before sundown you must gather all the grain that has been scattered. Then you may speak to me of marriage."

At that moment Kwelanga passed by on her way to the stream to draw water. She swayed gracefully beneath the earthen pot balanced on her head. When she saw the handsome suitor talking with her father, she began humming a little tune.

When the young man saw Kwelanga he thought she was as pretty as a sunbird. He said, "Let me begin at once."

Zamo went straight to the field. Finding a huge basket nearby, he took it and began picking up the kernels of kaffir corn. He worked all day without resting. When the sun was about to disappear in the west, he still hadn't finished half the field.

Just then he heard someone singing from the hillside above him:

> "Red grains of kaffir corn
> Scattered by our mothers,
> Fly back from whence you came,
> Gather with the others."

Suddenly the basket was heaped with grain. Zamo looked about and saw that the field was clean. He knew that every kernel had returned to the basket, and he carried the grain to Ngazulu.

When the chief saw the filled basket, he said, "You did well, young man. But that task was too easy. Tomorrow we shall talk again."

Zamo was given food and a hut in which to sleep. Very early the following morning he went to sit near the chief's door.

When Ngazulu came out, he said, "Young man, what do you want with me?"

Zamo said, "*Nkosi*, I have come to propose marriage at this *kraal*."

The chief said, "See that forest in the valley? If you are able to chop down all the trees before sunset, then come to me and talk of marriage."

Zamo fetched an axe and went to the forest. He set to work with all speed. Many trees fell before his axe. But the forest was large, and though he worked all day without resting, most of the trees were still left. As the sun was slipping behind the hill, he heard a sweet voice singing:

> "Trees of the forest,
> In the sun's red glow,
> Fall before Zamo—
> Bow yourselves low."

At that, the trees crashed down on every side. Not one was left standing. Just then the sun set. Zamo went to the chief and said, "*Nkosi*, have I not finished the task you gave me?"

The chief was very much surprised. He called his counselor and said, "Think of something really hard for this man to do. The tasks I have given him have been too easy."

The counselor put his hand over his mouth, as is the way with people in deep thought. Then he said, "Let Zamo come to us in the morning. We will think of something that is not so easy."

38

The chief and his counselor sat up all night discussing what trial to give the young man. Just as the sun was rising they came to a decision.

When Zamo appeared, the counselor said, "Young man, do you see that thorn tree growing out from the edge of the cliff—the one way up high on the mountainside? You are to climb out on it and pluck the topmost thorn."

Zamo saw the scraggly tree growing out from a crag high up on the mountain. No one could climb out on that, he thought. But he said nothing and set off up a steep mountain path.

The chief and his counselor watched him go. They were sure that Zamo would not be able to climb the tree because of the thorns. Even if he should manage to crawl out on it, the tree would bend with his weight and surely throw him off into the gorge. In any event, they thought they had seen the last of him.

When Zamo reached the edge of the cliff, he looked down to see what lay beneath the thorn tree. Far, far down he saw nothing but gray rubble—the rocks of all sizes that had rolled down the mountain. He knew that to fall would mean certain death.

The trunk of the thorn tree angled outward and upward from the edge of the cliff. Zamo began to creep out on it, picking his way between big thorns. As he neared the twisted umbrella of branches, the thorns were so close together that

39

there was no place even for fingertips. Then the tree began to bend. Zamo stopped breathing, and with great difficulty made his way back to the foot of the tree.

Just then he heard a voice singing behind him:

> "Thorn tree, thorn tree,
> Wind and weather worn tree,
> Your topmost thorn, please
> Pluck for Zamo and me."

Suddenly a small gray thorn came twirling through the air. It landed beside Zamo. He picked it up and, turning quickly, he saw Kwelanga coming toward him with outstretched hands. He knew at once that it was she who had sung the magic songs that had helped him every time.

Zamo took Kwelanga's hand, and together they went to her father.

"*Nkosi*," said Zamo, "here is the topmost thorn. I have finished the tasks. Kwelanga is willing, and I have come to propose marriage at this *kraal*."

When Ngazulu saw the look of happiness on the face of his daughter, he knew that Zamo truly was worthy of her. For he knew that the best husband for a woman is the man who can make her happy.

A Bantu Tale

Sebgugugu the Glutton

Sebgugugu was a poor man whose only possessions were a white cow named Gitale and her calf. One day while Tamme, his wife, was out hoeing in her garden plot in the forest, Sebgugugu sat in the sun in front of his house.

As he rested, a little bird alighted on the gatepost and began to sing. It twittered and warbled delightfully. And presently it seemed to Sebgugugu that it was singing words that he could understand. He thought he heard it sing:

> "Sebgugugu, kill Gitale.
> Kill Gitale and get a hundred."

When Tamme returned from the farm with the baby and the other two children at the end of the day, the bird was still nearby and still singing.

Sebgugugu said, "Listen, Tamme. Do you hear what that bird is saying?"

"Saying?" said Tamme. "It is only singing."

Sebgugugu said, "It is telling us that if we kill Gitale we shall get a hundred cows."

"Nonsense!" cried Tamme. "You are just hungry for meat. I have to feed our children on Gitale's milk. If you kill her, they will starve."

Sebgugugu said mysteriously, "I think Imana the Creator is sending us a message through that bird."

Tamme listened again as the bird sang. But she could hear no words. She begged Sebgugugu not to kill the cow. But he did. The family had meat for many days, but not even one cow appeared in place of Gitale.

One day the bird came again. This time it seemed to sing:

"Sebgugugu, kill the calf.
Kill the calf and get a hundred."

Sebgugugu killed the calf, but none came to replace it. Again the family ate meat for many days. When it was gone, they all became very hungry.

Then Sebgugugu put the baby into a basket which Tamme carried on her head. He took the other children by the

43

hand, one on either side, and they set out in search of food. They walked a long way without finding any at all. At last they sat down by the path to rest.

Then Sebgugugu cried out, "Imana, what shall we do?"

Imana heard and suddenly appeared before them. He pointed to a distant hill and said, "Beyond that hill is a cattle *kraal*. Go there and live on the milk from the cows. They are cared for by Igwababa, the crow. You must give him some of the milk, and never strike him or speak unkindly to him, for he is my faithful servant."

Sebgugugu and his family hurried on and soon came to the cattle *kraal*. There was no one there, but they found vessels full of milk. When Sebgugugu had drunk as much as he wanted, he gave his wife some, and she fed the children. Then they all sat down and waited to see what would happen.

When the sun was low, they saw the cattle coming. No herdboy ran along beside them. But a white-necked crow kept flying to and fro above them. The crow guided them into the cattlefold.

Sebgugugu and his household lived near that cattle *kraal* for several years. Then he became restless. One day he said, "Tamme, our children are big enough to herd cattle. I don't see what we want with that old crow. I shall kill him, and then the cows will belong to us."

Tamme begged him not to do anything so foolish. But

44

that evening Sebgugugu went out with his bow and arrow and lay in wait for the crow. When Igwababa came driving the cattle through the gate, he let the arrow fly. It missed, and the crow flew away. When Sebgugugu looked around, the cattle were nowhere to be seen. Not even one stray calf was left.

Once more the family had to set out in search of food. When they had walked all day without finding so much as one marula plum, Sebugugu cried out to Imana. This time the Creator led them to a wonderful vine with all kinds of fruits and vegetables growing on it. He said, "Pluck the fruits, but do not harm the vine."

The family lived off the bounty of the vine for many months. Then one day Sebgugugu said, "Tamme, that vine would produce more if I trimmed it."

Tamme begged him not to do it. But Sebgugugu never listened to his wife. He chopped off the dead branches, and the vine died.

Again the family was without food. Sebgugugu prayed to Imana for help. This time the Creator led them to a great rock with a crack in the middle of it. Out of the opening oozed porridge, beans, and many other kinds of food.

But the food came forth slowly. It took a long time to fill a basket. Sebgugugu said, "The crack is too narrow. I will make it wider." He sharpened one end of a big pole and hardened the tip of it in the fire. Then he thrust the point into the crack and pried with all his strength.

When Imana saw him do that, his patience was exhausted. He caused the crack to close up completely.

When Sebgugugu looked around, he found that his family was gone. They had disappeared without leaving a trace.

Sebgugugu, because of his greed, had lost all that he had.

A Thonga Tale

This for That

In an arid region south of the Limpopo River there was once a water hole where the wild animals came to drink. One morning when a rabbit came for water, he found not a drop.

An elephant came along. "I've come from the great forest, and I've found no water anywhere," he said.

Then a lion came. "M–m–m," he said. "So this water is gone too. We'll have to dig for it."

"I'll help," said the elephant. And he started at once to dig with his big front feet.

The lion and elephant worked fast and soon had dug a

deep hole. But all the rabbit did was slide down the heaps of sand which they piled up.

Soon water seeped into the hole. Then the lion said, "Go away, Rabbit. You wouldn't dig, so no water for you!"

"Oh, who wants water?" said the rabbit. And off he went. Soon he met an ostrich. "Oh, Ostrich," he cried, "the lion and the elephant have a well and they won't let me drink."

"Come with me, Rabbit," said the ostrich. "I will find us some watery berries." With his sharp eyes he soon found some berries. The two ate some and hid the rest in a hollow stump for another day. Then they went to their homes.

Later the rabbit went back to see if the berries were still in the stump. They were. "The ostrich won't know if I eat just one," he said.

He ate one. Then another and another. Soon he was eating them two at a time. Before long they were all gone. At that moment, along came the ostrich.

The rabbit didn't have time to hide. So he called out, "Oh, Ostrich, our berries are gone! Someone ate our berries."

The ostrich looked into the hollow stump. "If I find the one who ate them," he said, "I'll kick him to the moon."

The rabbit didn't want to be kicked, so he said, "You ate the berries! You are the only one who knew where they were."

"I did not!" cried the ostrich.

"Pay me for my berries!" said the rabbit.

49

"Pay for berries I didn't eat? I won't!" cried the ostrich. "Pay me with a feather," said the rabbit. "Then one of us will be happy."

"Oh, well," said the ostrich, "if a feather will make you happy, here." And he gave the rabbit a beautiful plume from his tail.

The rabbit went off chuckling softly to himself. Soon he came upon a man cooking a chunk of meat on a stick over a fire.

When the man saw the beautiful plume the rabbit was carrying, he said, "Let me feel that feather." He took it and ran his fingers over it. Then he put it on his head. Suddenly the wind caught the feather and tossed it into the fire. *Whish* went the fire, and the feather was gone.

The rabbit sang:

> "Oh, my feather is gone,
> The feather I got for my berries,
> The berries that are all eaten up.
> Oh, now I have nothing."

"Don't be sad, Little Rabbit," said the man. "I'll give you my meat."

So the rabbit took the meat and went on his way. Soon he met a woman who was carrying a bowl of sour milk on her head. "Will you give me that meat for this good sour milk?" she asked.

"No," said the rabbit. "But you make a fire and heat the meat, and I will let you eat it with me. I will sleep under this tree, and you must call me when the meat is ready."

The rabbit lay down and went to sleep. When the meat was hot, the woman ate it all herself. When the rabbit awoke he saw that nothing was left but the bone. He sang:

> "Oh, my meat is gone,
> The meat I got for my feather,
> The feather I got for my berries,
> The berries that are all eaten up.
> Oh, now I have nothing."

"Here," said the woman, "take my sour milk instead."

So the rabbit took the sour milk and went on his way. But he didn't want the milk. He said to himself, "How can I get rid of this sour milk? Someone will have to pay for it."

Soon he came to a large ant hill. "I know," he said, "the ants will pay for my sour milk." Up the ant hill he went. Near the top he slipped. The milk slopped out, and he and the bowl rolled down the hill.

The ant queen came out of one of the doorways. The rabbit said, "See what your hill did!" Then he sang:

> "Oh, my sour milk is gone,
> The milk I got for my meat,
> The meat I got for my feather,

The feather I got for my berries,
The berries that are all eaten up.
Oh, now I have nothing."

The ant queen said to her workers, "Fill his bowl with winged ants." And they did.

The rabbit set off with the bowl of winged ants. "The lion will like these," he said. "Now I will go to the well and get water." He hurried back to the well and found the lion there.

"Look, Lion," he said. "See what I have? Winged ants! I'll give them to you for some water."

"Go away," growled the lion. "You would not dig. Besides, Elephant would be mad if I let you have some."

"I know how to trick Elephant," said the rabbit. "You pretend to sleep. And I'll tie you up. Then you can say that you couldn't stop me."

Now the lion did like winged ants. But he didn't like to catch them one by one. He looked at the bowl full of them and said, "Tie me up, Rabbit."

The rabbit did. As he worked, the lion asked, "Where did you get all those ants?"

"From the ant queen, to pay for my sour milk," said the rabbit.

"What sour milk?" asked the lion.

"The milk I got for my meat."

"What meat?"

"The meat I got for my feather."

"What feather?"

"The feather I got from Ostrich to pay for the berries he didn't eat."

"What?" cried the lion.

"I ate them and I told him *he* did," laughed the rabbit.

Then out of the bush came the ostrich. His wings were spread so he looked three times his size. "Ho! So it was you who ate the berries!" he cried.

"Don't kick me! Don't kick me!" begged the rabbit. "I'll pay you for the berries. I'll pay you with these good winged ants."

"No!" roared the lion. "You won't pay him with *my* winged ants."

"I didn't give them to you yet," said the rabbit.

"Give them to me now!" roared the lion.

But the rabbit gave the ants to the ostrich. Then he ran to the well and began to drink.

When the lion saw him do that, he gave a terrible roar.

The rabbit was so scared he fell into the well. "Help!" he cried.

The ostrich reached his long neck down into the water and plucked him out. Then he sat down and let the rabbit climb onto his back with the bowl of winged ants.

At that moment, the elephant came out of the bush.

54

"Elephant," cried the lion, "get me away from this tree. I want to catch that rabbit."

"I don't know how to get a lion away from a tree. But I know how to get a tree away from a lion," said the elephant. Then he pulled up the tree. But the lion was still tied fast to it.

Now the ostrich ran down the path with the rabbit on his back. After them came the elephant carrying the tree with the roaring, kicking lion on it.

"Don't let them get me," begged the rabbit.

The ostrich looked back. "With that load, Elephant can't run at all," he said.

Soon the ostrich and the rabbit were far ahead of their pursuers. The rabbit was so happy he said, "I'll give you all of my winged ants, Ostrich. And I'll give you a hug, besides."

He snuggled against the big bird's skinny neck. And as he did, away went the bowl. And away went the ants—all over the path!

A Zulu Tale

Tusi and the Great Beast

There was once a Zulu village so large that it looked like many villages put together. It was ruled by a king named Amuntu.

King Amuntu had a beautiful daughter named Tusi. When she came of age, she was secluded in an umgonqo hut to be prepared for marriage. Because Tusi had often walked with her father among the cattle, he decided to obtain a herd of cows as a present for her on the day when she came forth.

So the royal army was sent on a cattle raid. The soldiers came upon a herd of cows grazing in a distant valley. There were black and brown cows and some splotched with white.

The soldiers were delighted. Best of all, there were no men or boys guarding the herd.

However, overlooking the valley was a great beast named Mapundu. He was so large that rivers and forests, hills and valleys were on his back. He was so long that at the south end of him it was winter, and at the north end early harvest.

The soldiers thought Mapundu was merely a range of hills. They began at once to drive off the cattle. Mapundu thundered, "Stop! Those cows are mine!"

But Amuntu's soldiers were not to be stopped with words. They only hurried the faster, and soon they had Mapundu's herd well on the way to their village.

On the day that Tusi was to be brought forth from the umgonqo hut, all the people went to the royal gardens for the ceremony. Only Tusi and a maidservant stayed behind. They were to come later.

Tusi had just finished putting on her brass ornaments and her beaded calfskin dress when the heavens thundered. She looked out and saw the great beast standing at the entrance to the village.

Mapundu cleared his throat. The thunder rolled across the sky. Then he bellowed, "Princess, come forth and climb upon my back!"

Tusi was afraid to obey, but more afraid not to. With trembling hands she gathered up her brass pillow, her sleeping mat, and her rod, and climbed up onto the back of the

beast. Then Mapundu set out at great speed.

The maidservant ran and told the king. He sent his soldiers in pursuit. They overtook the beast and rained their spears upon him. But the spears fell into the forests and did not stab anything. At last the men turned back.

Mapundu took Tusi to a far-off land. He put her down beside a cave carved from rock which sparkled in the sun. A mealie patch spread out before the cave. Mapundu said, "You will live here and pluck food for yourself." With that he rushed off.

Tusi walked in the garden and picked some corn. Then she sat down in the doorway of the cave. Soon she saw a very thin man approaching from over a hill. He hopped in a most curious way.

Tusi hid herself in the back room of the cave. Presently she heard the snapping sound of mealie cobs being plucked. Then the stranger came hopping into the cave. Tusi extended her hands around the corner of the inner wall. When the man saw those hands, he fled. Tusi peeked out and saw that he was a Lungulebe, a half-man. He had one leg, one arm, and half of everything else.

The Lungulebe went to his chief and said, "There are people in Mapundu's cave. There are two of them."

The next day a company of Lungulebe went to the cave. The chief called, "Step forth, whoever you are!"

Tusi thought, Now I shall be killed. But I shall die like

the daughter of a king. She put on her beaded garment and carried her rod and pillow of brass.

When she came out, the chief cried, "Look! A double woman. Two arms, two legs. She would be pretty except for those two legs!"

The Lungulebe laughed and laughed at Tusi. Then they took her to their village. The chief gave her one of his royal houses, and he called her his daughter. He sent a gift of cattle to Mapundu to pay for the right to keep her.

Tusi was treated so well and fed so much that she became very fat. When she became too fat to walk, the chief's counselors said, "Let the two-legged one be eaten and her fat melted down. Of what use is a person who can no longer walk?"

The chief agreed. A huge hole was dug and a fire built in it. Then a great pot was placed upon the fire. When it was red hot, the counselors carried Tusi to it.

On the way to her death, Tusi looked up into the bright sky and sang:

> "Listen, Heaven! Hear my plea!
> Save me from the fire of the Lungulebe!"

Suddenly a great storm burst upon them. The rain poured down and put out the fire. The pot burst into a hundred pieces. Lightning stabbed here and there, killing the chief and many of the people.

Only a few remained. They said, "Let us never touch her again. But let us begrudge her food until she dies."

Tusi was glad to have but little food. She soon became thin. Then one day she put all her things into a basket, set it on her head, and started out to find her home. She journeyed alone, sleeping in the open country.

After many days Tusi found her father's village. King Amuntu was sitting at the gate, with his hair grown long as a sign of grief. At once he had it cut and he put on a new head-ring, for happiness had returned to his household.

When it became known that Tusi had returned, many chiefs asked to marry her. But to all, King Amuntu gave the same answer: "Tusi was saved from Mapundu and the Lungulebe. Now she shall never leave me."

It happened that there was a chief in a distant land who heard about the beautiful princess who could not be bought with a bride price. He sent a wise old counselor to fetch her. The old man turned himself into a frog and came leaping into the village of King Amuntu.

The people gathered around it saying, "What a beautiful frog!"

Tusi caught it and took it to her hut. Then the frog said, "Get your things and come with me."

Tusi put all her treasures into a basket, put it on her head, and followed the frog out of the village. When they had traveled a short distance, the frog turned back into an old man. He told Tusi that he had come to fetch her to be the bride of his chief.

After they had gone a great distance the old man looked at Tusi and said, "Why should I fetch such a lovely creature as you for someone else? I shall take you to another place and keep you for myself."

Tusi did not want to be the wife of that old man. She stood still and said, "My head, open for me." The top of her head opened and she put all her things into it—even the basket. Then her head closed, but it was fearfully large. After that the man said no more about wanting her for himself.

At length they reached the village of the chief. The old man bowed and said, "Oh Chief, I have fetched the woman you wanted. But her head is not right."

The people gathered around. They said, "The maiden's head is deformed. Let her be sent away."

The chief's sister said, "Brother, let her stay. Even if you do not marry her."

So Tusi stayed. And the people called her Ukandakulu, which means big head.

One day the chief's sister went with Tusi to bathe in the river. She asked, "What caused your head to become so big?"

Tusi said, "All my things are in it." Then she rolled her eyes upward and said, "My head, open for me." Her head opened. She tipped it and let the things fall to the ground, even the basket. At once her head closed and became small.

When the chief saw Tusi with her head the proper size, he was pleased. At once he arranged to have cattle taken to her father to pay the bride price. The two were married. And Tusi reigned happily with her husband for many years.

A Tshindao Tale

Saso and Gogwana the Witch

Long ago near the Zambesi River there lived a poor man with his wife and six children. With so many mouths to feed, often there was scarcely enough food to give everyone a taste. And one day they had nothing to eat at all. They decided to look for food on the other side of the river.

When they reached the riverbank, they found the waters in full flood. The wife said, "*Baba*, what shall we do? The river is deep and angry, and the children can't swim!"

The father said, "I shall carry them across." One by one he managed to get the four smallest ones safely to the other side. The mother crossed by herself. But Saso and Moya, the oldest son and oldest daughter, were left behind with Phiri, the dog, to protect them.

Saso, Moya, and the dog began at once to follow a path that ran alongside the river. At length they happened upon an endless line of ants carrying kernels of grain.

"Let's see where they've come from," said Saso. The procession of ants led them to a cave which was filled with baskets of grain.

"We're rich!" cried Moya. She found stones suitable for grinding, and in a short time had porridge cooking.

The two lived in the cave for many days. Then Saso became restless. He left Moya in the cave and set out with the dog to see what he could find.

The next day Saso came upon a dead buffalo on the forest path. Phiri sniffed it, but did not try to eat it. So Saso did not cut any meat from it. He knew that the dog was wise about what was not safe for eating.

At length Saso and Phiri came to a village which was inhabited only by women and girls. Saso learned that the witch, Gogwana, lived in the Great House there. She had eaten all the men and boys, except for a few who had escaped into the forest.

The women begged Saso to run for his life. But when the big, ugly Gogwana came waddling out of her house and invited him to come in and eat, he went in. Luckily his dog followed at his heels.

Gogwana cooked porridge in one pot and meat in another. While the porridge was cooking, she secretly threw in a little poison. She put the food down before Saso, saying, "Eat it, my grandson."

Saso first slipped a piece of meat to Phiri. The dog gobbled it up, so Saso ate the meat. But when Phiri refused even to taste the porridge, the boy didn't eat any of it either.

Gogwana said, "Grandson, eat your porridge. It's good for you."

Saso thought a moment, then he said, "In my country it is the custom sometimes to eat only meat."

At the end of the day the witch called Saso to another meal. This time the dog ate the porridge but refused to touch the meat. So the boy ate only porridge.

"Yini! Now you eat the porridge and not the meat!" cried Gogwana.

"In my country," said Saso, "at other times we eat only porridge."

The witch was furious. But she hid her anger and handed the boy a sleeping mat. "Good night, Grandson," she said sweetly. "You sleep on that side of the fire."

Saso spread the mat and lay down with the dog nestled beside him.

Now Gogwana only pretended to sleep. When she was sure that Saso was sleeping, she took a cooking stone and crept toward him, intending to hit him on the head.

But the dog heard her coming. He sprang up and clamped his teeth on the old woman's wrist. She dropped the stone and screamed, "Call off your dog!"

Saso pulled the dog away. Then he said, "Old woman, stay away from me, or Phiri will bite you again. And next time I'll let him!" Then he quieted the dog, and they lay down and slept.

In the morning Saso and Phiri went for a walk while Gogwana cooked breakfast. As soon as they were out of sight, the witch dug a deep pit in front of the door. Then she covered it with a mat and sprinkled sand over it.

When Saso and Phiri returned, she called them to come in and eat. Now the dog was running ahead up the path to the Great House. When he had almost reached the door, he stopped and turned aside. He ran around to the side of the house and leaped in through the window. So the boy also entered through the window.

"Ɔini!" cried the witch. "Why did you come through the window?"

"That is the custom at our house," said Saso. "Sometimes we climb through the window."

"Eat your porridge, then," said Gogwana. The dog ate it, so the boy did, too. Between them they ate it all. Then they left by way of the window.

Before the evening meal, the witch dug a pit under the window and covered it with a mat and some dry grass. When

70

the food was ready, she called, "Come, Grandson. Come and eat."

Again the dog ran ahead. He had almost reached the window, when he turned sharply and trotted back to his master. The boy stayed where he was and called out, "Grandmother, I am not hungry!"

The witch put her ugly head out the door. "You're lying," she scolded. "People are always hungry at mealtime."

"At our house," said Saso, "sometimes we are not hungry."

The witch grumbled to herself. Then she called, "Grandson, come along with me to fetch firewood." She came out carrying an axe. She insisted that the dog be left tied to the gatepost.

So Saso tied Phiri and followed after the witch by himself. The dog didn't like being tied, and he began at once to chew on the rope.

Saso and the witch had not gone far when they came to a dying tree. Gogwana told the boy to climb it and chop branches off the top. As soon as he was high in the tree, she cried out, "I have you now. And I'm going to kill you!" With that, she began biting the tree with her sharp teeth.

"Phiri! Phiri! Phiri!" screamed Saso at the top of his voice.

The dog heard him. With one jerk he broke the last strand of the rope and came bounding up just as the tree was about to fall. He seized the witch by her ankle and dragged her away from the tree.

Then Saso climbed down and killed her with one blow of the axe.

Just then down from the sky flew a great bird. It alighted on a nearby rock. It was so huge that had it settled in a tree, the tree would have broken beneath it. The bird bellowed, "I am Mapimbiro, the son of Gogwana. You have killed my mother!"

Mapimbiro made a flying leap toward Saso. But Phiri rushed between. And the bird caught the dog in its talons instead.

Then Saso swung the axe with all his strength and killed the big bird. Afterward he built a great fire and burned the witch and her strange child.

When Saso returned to the village and told the women and girls what he had done, they danced about him shouting, "Be our chief! Be our chief!"

So Saso became chief of the village. The men and boys who were in hiding came back to live with their families. A messenger, with Phiri to guide him, fetched Moya from the cave. Later, the father and mother and other sisters and brothers were also found. And they all lived happily in Saso's village for many years.

73

A Zulu Tale

The House in the Middle
of the Road

There was once a widow named Unanana who lived with her two small children in a house in the middle of the road. The road flowed around the house on either side, so it was like an island in the middle of a river.

One morning Unanana went out to hunt for wild potatoes, leaving the children in the care of a young girl named Nontando.

Unanana told the girl that if any animals threatened the children, she should tell them, "These are the children of Unanana. They are protected by her magic power." She reminded her that if any Abatwa happened along, she should greet them with the words: "I saw you a long way off."

Nontando knew that the Abatwa are people no larger than the fingers of a man. They hide in the grass and shoot men with their tiny poison arrows. However, they are embarrassed by their small size. So if anyone says he has seen them from afar, the Abatwa will feel flattered and will be friendly.

Unanana was no sooner out of sight than a baboon came along. He said, "Whose fat children are those?"

"They belong to Unanana," said Nontando. "They are protected by her magic power."

"They are beautiful," said the baboon. "If they were not Unanana's, I would carry them off." Then he swung off around one side of the house, walking on the knuckles of his hands and the soles of his feet.

Soon a leopard came by, and then a lion. Both asked the same question. To each Nontando gave the same answer. Both animals said they would have eaten the children, were they not protected by the power of Unanana.

At midday there came along a brown horse with a hundred Abatwa on his back, sitting one behind the other from mane to tail. Each carried a tiny bow, and wore a quiver of arrows on his shoulder.

Nontando ran out to meet them, calling out, "Greetings, Abatwa! I saw you as you came over the hill."

The little people were pleased that anyone could see them from so great a distance. They stopped their horse long

enough to visit for a moment, then went on.

Late in the day there came a great elephant with only one tusk. He asked, "Whose children are those?"

Nontando said, "They are the children of Unanana. They are protected by her magic power."

"What do I care about her magic power?" bellowed the elephant. And with that, he swallowed both children. Then he looked around for Nontando. He would have swallowed her too, if she had not shinnied up a tree just in time.

When Unanana returned with a skin bag filled with potatoes, she asked, "Where are my children?"

Nontando said, "Oh, a great elephant with one tusk swallowed them. He would have eaten me too, but I escaped up a tree."

"Which way did he go?" asked Unanana.

Nontando pointed down the road behind the house. "That way," she said.

Unanana hastily filled a pot with *amasi*, which she carried on her head. Then she took up her knife and set out. Soon she came upon the Abatwa. The tiny people were camping for the night near a large ant hill. They were crawling in and out of the ant burrows, looking for places to sleep.

Unanana said, "Greetings! I saw you from a long way off. Can you tell me where to find an elephant with one tusk? He has swallowed my children, and I must find him."

The chief of the Abatwa said, "Go on until you come to

the land where the trees are high and the stones are white."

At length, Unanana came upon the lion, the leopard, and then the baboon. She asked them each the same question. They all told her to keep going until she reached the place where the trees were tall and the stones were white.

The woman traveled all night. As the sun was rising, she saw that she had come to the land of tall trees and white stones. She looked about her and there, under a tree, she saw a huge elephant.

Unanana hurried to it and said, "Elephant, tell me where to find the elephant with one tusk, and I will give you this bowl of *amasi*."

The animal turned around, and Unanana saw that one of its tusks was missing. She cried, "You are the one who swallowed my children!"

The elephant opened his huge mouth and lunged for the woman. He swallowed her, the knife, and even the bowl of *amasi*.

When Unanana reached the stomach of the beast she found trees, plants, people, dogs, and goats that had been swallowed. And sitting under a bush, all huddled together, were her own children. She fed them the *amasi*, for they were very hungry.

Then Unanana took her knife and cut a great slit between the rib bones of the elephant. The beast fell dead, and people and dogs and goats rushed out of the opening.

When Unanana returned home with her children, Nontando was delighted. She had thought that she would never see them again.

The other people who had escaped from inside the elephant were so happy to be free that for days they kept bringing gifts to the house in the middle of the road. So Unanana and her children became very rich.

Glossary

Aardvark / The aardvark is a great digger. In a very short time, it can burrow into the earth to escape an enemy. With its sharp claws the aardvark rips open the nests of ants and termites, then catches those insects with its long, sticky tongue.

Aardwolf / An animal of South Africa which looks somewhat like a hyena. Its back slopes down from shoulders to tail, and its reddish fur is striped with black. Because of its small teeth, it eats only very small animals and insects.

Amasi / Curds of clotted milk, similar to cottage cheese.

Baba / Father.

Biltong / Meat cut into strips and dried in the sun.

Great House / Home of the chief.

Great Wife / First wife.

Gwenye tree / Also called Kaffir plum. It has rough bark, red leaves, and red fruit.

Head-ring / A sort of crown made by rolling together the midribs of palm fronds and entwining them into the hair.

Heyi / A salutation, such as *hi* or *hello*.

Imana / Bantu name for God, the Creator.

Kaffir corn / A grain first cultivated by the Kaffirs of South Africa. The plant has a stout stalk with long broad leaves growing from it and a thick bunch of seeds at the tip of each stalk. The seedheads contain about as many seeds as cobs of maize, but the seeds do not grow on corncobs. Each red kernel is attached by a tiny stem.

Kwowu / An exclamation used for emphasis.

Kraal / A circle of beehive-shaped huts of the Zulu household arranged around a cattle *kraal*—which is a circular space enclosed by a thorn fence.

Lungfish / A very primitive fish which breathes with lungs as well as with gills.

Marula plum / A tree which grows wild in the grassland of South Africa. It has grayish, mottled bark and succulent fruit resembling plums. The pits, or seeds, of the marula plums are edible, and are sometimes used to make an intoxicating drink.

Mealie patch / Corn (maize) patch.

Mountains of the Dragon / The Drakensberg Mountains.

Nkosi / Chief.

Phiri / Wolf.

Umgonqo hut / A small hut or chamber erected inside a house.

Yini / An expression meaning *What is this?*

Sources of the Stories

I am indebted to librarians Florence Harnau and Demeras Roen for combing libraries in four states for material for this book.

"Little Hen Eagle" is retold from "Untombi-Yapansi" in *Nursery Tales, Traditions, and Histories of the Zulus, in Their Own Words, with a Translation into English*, Vol. I., by the Rev. Canon Henry Callaway, M.D., published by Trubner & Co., London, 1868.

"The Trick on the Trek" is retold from "Crocodile's Treason" in *South African Folk-Tales* by J. A. Honey, published by Baker and Taylor Co., The Trow Press, New York, 1910.

"Tshinyama's Heavenly Maidens" is retold from two stories: "Skin-sore and the Heavenly Maidens" and "The Healing of Skin-sore" in *The Bull of the Kraal and the Heavenly Maidens* by Dudley Kidd, published by Adam and Charles Black, London, 1908.

"How Blue Crane Taught Jackal to Fly" is retold from "Jackal and Dove" in *Lion and Jackal with Other Folk Tales from South Africa* by Frank Brownlee, published by George Allen & Unwin, London, 1938.

"The Winning of Kwelanga" is retold from "The Story of Mzamo" in *Lion and Jackal with Other Folk Tales from South Africa* by Frank Brownlee, published by George Allen & Unwin, London, 1938.

"Sebgugugu the Glutton" is retold from a story beginning on page 45 in *Myths and Legends of the Bantu* by Alice Werner, published by George G. Harrap & Co., London, 1933.

"This for That" is retold from J. Torrend's "Master Rabbit and the Berries" in *Specimens of Bantu Folk-Lore from Northern Rhodesia*, published by Routledge & Kegan Paul, London, 1921.

"Tusi and the Great Beast" is retold from "Umkxakaza-Wako-gingqwayo" in *Nursery Tales, Traditions, and Histories of the Zulus, in Their Own Words, with a Translation into English*, Vol. I., by the Rev. Canon Henry Callaway, M.D., published by Trubner & Co., London, 1868.

"Saso and Gogwana the Witch" is retold from "How Skin-sore killed a Cannibal" in *The Bull of the Kraal and the Heavenly Maidens* by Dudley Kidd, published by Adam and Charles Black, London, 1908.

84

"The House in the Middle of the Road" is retold from "Unanana-Bosele" in *Nursery Tales, Traditions, and Histories of the Zulus, in Their Own Words, with a Translation into English*, Vol. I., by the Rev. Canon Henry Callaway, M.D., published by Trubner & Co., London, 1868.